P9-BYT-288

The Forty Fathom Bank

The Forty Fathom Bank

NOVELLA BY LES GALLOWAY

CHRONICLE BOOKS
SAN FRANCISCO

Printed in the United States of America.

Library of Congress Cataloging-in-Publication Data

Galloway, Les.
    The forty fathom bank : novella / by Les Galloway.
       p.   cm.
    ISBN 0-8118-0034-2 (hc)
    I. Title. II. Title: Forty fathom bank.
  [PS3557.A4156F6   1994]
  813'.54--dc20   93-26071
                                 CIP

Book and cover design: Brenda Rae Eno
Composition: On Line Typography

Distributed in Canada by Raincoast Books,
112 East Third Avenue
Vancouver B. C. V5T 1C8

10 9 8 7 6 5 4 3 2 1

Chronicle Books
275 Fifth Street
San Francisco, CA 94103

And when he finds that the sum of his transgressions is great he will many a time like a child start up in his sleep, and he is filled with dark forebodings.

—Plato, *The Republic*

1

1 1 1

FOR THE FIRST FEW months I felt nothing, really, except now and then a vague feeling of uneasiness like the after-effect of a dream whose full meaning has escaped in the dark fragments of its own confused scenes. Beyond that, it seldom crossed my mind, and when it did I would tell myself that it was an accident, an accident at sea. I would say it over and over again, like an incantation, and try not to think of anything but the words. That way, I was able to keep it locked up inside me, concealed, so to speak, from my conscious thoughts. And too, I managed to keep myself quite busy, much busier than I needed to be, so that I had little time for reflection.

But one night after all my business was done, when everything was in perfect order, I woke up out of a sound sleep. I just opened my eyes and was wide awake in the middle of the night. After that, nothing did any good.

Now all this was a long time ago, so it would seem only natural that the whole experience, as terrible as it was, should eventually have faded from my mind. But nothing has changed. The old feelings of uneasiness have settled in permanently. Though I have tried a thousand devices to keep them at bay, they slip in without any warning, anywhere, anytime at all, but especially when I happen to be around the docks or small boats or whenever the dank low water smell of the Bay or the ocean catch me off guard—feelings that have gathered a kind of cloudy horror about them as the years go by. And every now and then the memory of Ethan May, faceless as in a dream, slips like a shadow across my mind.

We were living in San Francisco at the time. We still live here. In spite of everything, it is a difficult city to leave. Yet sometimes I think I should have taken the family and moved inland, away from the coast and the water and all the associations: the unpredictable reminders that unleash the hordes of silent apprehensions hidden away in the deepest recesses of my consciousness.

But decisions have always come hard, mainly I suppose because I've never been sure of things. Nor of myself. I was twenty-eight then, nervous, thin, tired all the time and suffering from a kind of hopelessness of spirit I firmly believe came from having been reared by a godfearing grandmother. Her countless tales of fire and damnation, along with a very realistic and abiding fear of poverty had, since my earliest childhood, filled me with gloom and confusion. I learned very young to be afraid of both God and his inscrutable wrath, and of the struggle to survive without money. Goaded by threats of punishment, I recited my prayers, but always with the hope they'd be answered not with guidance or forgiveness, but with money, which even as a child I found more effective in exorcising the evils of this world than the whispered appeals for divine approval.

My grandmother died at eighty-two, sustained to the last by fantasies of eternal bliss in the Four Square City of Gold and a life-long confidence in the Second Coming, but leaving me with nothing but a legacy of self-doubt and confusion to face the worst years of the depression.

I had nothing, and as I look back it seems that I must have accepted this fact as my way of life, though resentfully and with considerable fear. And being afraid, I took few chances. I clung to things, to the status quo, to my wife, my jobs, and I avoided changes.

Yet sometime before the war, I did something quite

unusual for me. I acquired an old fishing boat. I say acquired because no one in those days, or certainly no one I knew, could afford to buy anything but essentials. It was a big boat, nearly sixty feet long and quite seaworthy despite its weathered look, with a fifteen-ton hold and deck space for a good many tons more. The capacity of the boat, however, had little bearing on its value, for fish at that time brought such a low price that it hardly paid to go out after them.

The boat, called the Blue Fin, was part of an estate, and since no one wanted it, I came by it for something like five hundred dollars, to be paid over an indefinite period of time. My intention was to put a railing around it and take out fishing parties on weekends to augment my twenty-five dollars a week income in a real estate office which was always about to go out of business.

Of course, I had another idea in buying the Blue Fin, and that was to move aboard with my family on that inevitable day when I couldn't pay the rent on the tiny apartment we were squeezed into, that little prison with its dark, unventilated rooms, its lines of damp clothes in the kitchen and where my two kids woke up to life playing on the bare floors, or outside on the dirty street beneath the endless gray of our San Francisco summers.

As it turned out, the real estate office did not go

out of business, but for some reason I was let go anyway. However, by the time I received my last check I had managed, with energy born of desperate necessity, since I knew nothing about boats then, to get the Blue Fin in shape and was already running a few fishing parties to partially compensate for the loss of my job.

And this was my life for more than three years, shivering on the dock at two and three o'clock in the fog-wet mornings waiting for a party of firemen or policemen or office workers who sometimes showed up and sometimes didn't. And on the days, and there were more than enough of them, when the boat lay idle I would clean or paint or work on the engine or go around to the bait shops drumming up business.

It was on those no income days as I used to call them, depressed and tired, I would often watch the husky, leathery-skinned Sicilians returning—laughing that good, high-pitched, prolonged laughter that came up from their guts, shouting and cajoling each other from their little blue and white clipper-bowed crab boats—those crafty, warm, loud, strong people who could eke a living from the sea and prosper because they were born to it, because their blood and bones and muscles and stomachs and temperaments were adapted for centuries to it. And comparing myself to them I began to believe that my physical frailness—I was five eleven and not much over one hundred and forty pounds—was bound up with our continued poverty.

This thought obsessed me so much I began to have fantasies of doing something wild and dangerous like running Chinamen in from Mexico at five hundred dollars a head or smuggling jewels or even heroin.

Probably I'd still be at it, or something equally profitless, had it not been for the strange and fortuitous business of the sharks that struck the California coast in the fall of 1940 and that, in little more than a year, found me richer than I'd ever dreamed possible.

2

* * *

I SAID IT BEGAN in 1940. Actually, that whole dreamlike affair that changed the lives of so many of us, had been building up for some time, ever since the Nazis had invaded Scandinavia and cut off the exportation of North Sea fish and especially of fish liver oil—a vital source of Vitamin A which, at the time, could not be made synthetically. With the threat of a global war hanging over us, neither the cod fisheries in New England nor the halibut catch off the North Pacific coast could begin to fill the demand.

Now all this, it might seem, would have had little bearing on the fishing industry along the California coast where cod are not plentiful and halibut even less so. And since there were no other known fishes which could supply the needed Vitamin, it should follow that a windfall from the sea would be highly unlikely.

But one day in the late fall, a small boat pulled up to the Acme Fish Company dock at Fisherman's Wharf. The fishermen had been set-lining for rock fish, but, unfortunately, had run into a school of small gray nurse sharks locally called soupfins because the Chinese use the fins for soup. Aside from that small market, the fish were worthless and considered a pest. And it was only out of sympathy for the fisherman that the buyer contributed five dollars a ton for the catch. His intention, no doubt, was to recoup his loss by selling the carcasses for chicken feed. Two days later that same buyer called the fisherman and offered him fifteen dollars a ton for all he could bring in.

Of course, the news of such generosity spread quickly and it was soon discovered that the buyer for Acme had, and for no other reason than pure curiosity, sent samples of shark liver to the government laboratory for analysis. The results showed the Vitamin A concentrate to be sixteen times greater than that of a prime cod. Furthermore, a report from the State Bureau of Fisheries disclosed that the soupfin's liver averaged something like fifteen percent of the fish's entire body weight! Overnight the price shot up to fifty dollars. By the end of November when the sharks disappeared for the winter, they were bringing seventy-five dollars per ton.

Naturally, the big question in everyone's mind was whether or not they were going to stay at seventy-five. There was much talk around the Wharf. Some speculated it might go up to one hundred; others were convinced it was a result of war hysteria and that by spring when the sharks showed up again, they'd be down to their original nothing. But even the most pessimistic, I noticed, were laying in coils of quarter inch manila line. And there was a sudden shortage of shark hooks in all the supply houses.

Here was my chance, I thought. With spring over four months away, I'd have plenty of time to get ready. I talked to my wife.

"Isn't it dangerous?" she asked.

"No more so than taking out parties," I replied, though at the time, I had almost no idea of what was involved.

"We sure could use the money," she said, plaintively.

There was no doubt about that, I thought, and began immediately to make plans for converting the Blue Fin to shark fishing. I checked the other boats, talked to fishermen, made sketches of the Blue Fin's deck and hold. I even sent away to the National Bureau of Fisheries for all the available literature on sharks, their breeding and migratory habits.

It turned out to be a bigger job than I had thought.
The equipment was expensive. The power gurdy that was
needed to pull in the fish would have cost more than three
hundred dollars. There were coils of manila line to be
bought, several thousand hooks plus anchors and floats
and hard twist cotton for leaders or ganions as they're
called. Any one of a dozen fish buyers would have fi-
nanced me, I knew. But what if the price of sharks went
down to nothing again, I wondered anxiously. What if the
boat were impounded for debt?

Winter came on with its week-long rains inter-
spersed with southwest gales that whipped the ocean to
a foaming frenzy. Except for some net mending between
storms and the usual fleet of intrepid little crab boats that
went chunking out in the two A.M. blackness, the Wharf
was deserted. Beneath the enervating cover of cold gray
skies, the autumn vision of sudden riches from shark livers and Vitamin A soon faded.

The first boat to catch any sharks the following
spring was the Viking with two men aboard, Karl Hansen and his brother Jon. They had been fishing on Cordell
Bank which is about fifty miles northwest of the Gate.
After just two days they returned with ten tons in their
hold. News of the catch created a quick resurgence of excitement. When the Viking tied up at the Union Fish

Company's dock most everyone around hurried down to see what kind of price the sharks would bring.

"I'll bet they don't get over twenty dollars," I remember Joe La Rocca saying.

"Hell they might not even buy 'em," someone else said.

Secretly I hoped he was right. For, though I desperately needed the money, I still could not face the risks involved, the uncertainties and complications. I felt safe with things the way they were. But I'm sure no one in that crowd of hungry fishermen shared my feelings. A ruddy glow diffused their heavy Sicilian cheeks: their clear, dark, predatory eyes looked on with hawklike alertness. In that atmosphere of greedy expectancy, where the smell of fish entrails mingled with the tang of creosoted pilings and the heavy garlic breath of the fishermen, only one man, a shadowy observer, appeared detached from the whole tense scene. I do not remember what he looked like, only that a feeling of quiescence seemed to emanate from where he was standing, alone, in a far corner of the shed.

Nothing happened until late in the afternoon when half a dozen of the biggest fish buyers in town showed up. With them was a man in a gray business suit whom no one had ever seen before. The twenty or more fishermen who gathered stayed together talking quietly in Italian. Then Karl Hansen, the Viking's owner, climbed up on a box and asked for bids.

"Holy Christ," Joe shouted, "they're going to auction them off."

Tarantino started the bidding at twenty dollars.

"That's about what I figured," someone said, gloomily, "the whole thing was too damned good to be true."

But just then the man in the gray suit said he'd go one hundred.

"He must be off his rocker," Joe said, "or else there's something going on we don't know about."

After that we just stood there with our mouths open, staring, as the bids jumped from two hundred to five hundred to seven hundred.

"Anybody go eight?" Karl Hansen asked tensely.

The man in the gray suit raised his hand then immediately took out his check book and those of us who were close enough saw him hurriedly write out a check for eight thousand dollars. Printed on the check was the name of one of the biggest pharmaceutical houses in the country.

The next minute every fisherman in the place was running for his boat, that is, everyone but me. I was too sick at heart, too filled with despair to care about anything.

After a time I walked down to the Blue Fin and sat, disconsolately, in the wheelhouse. Where would it all end, I wondered, close to tears. Why was it that I alone was always singled out for failure? I looked out at the Blue Fin's big afterdeck, at the stout sideboards and the heavy planked hatch cover and thought of the big empty fish hold below. Suddenly my despair turned to anger.

"If you'd get off your dead ass and do something," I said to myself, "you could pull out of this mess in no time. Borrow the money, outfit the boat and get the hell out there before you blow it again."

It was the same kind of thinking that had jolted me into buying the boat in the first place and then into taking out parties. Now, as if I had been brutally slapped into consciousness, the prospects loomed, not only enormous, but easily attainable. Then, as if this wasn't enough to stimulate me to action, just as I was leaving the Wharf I met Joe La Rocca unloading his pick-up.

"You heard the latest?" he asked, excitedly and, without waiting for a reply, "Some nut up in Eureka is paying eighteen hundred dollars a ton," he shouted, jubilantly, "so they've pegged the price at eighteen hundred all along the coast. Think of it," he cried, pounding me on the back, "That's damned near a dollar a pound for them stinkin' sharks."

Perhaps all this was too much for me. Perhaps I didn't really believe it. One way or the other I did nothing. And the weeks passed. I made plans to borrow the money and convert the Blue Fin. I talked to fishermen, learned where they'd caught their sharks, studied their fishing gear. I became an expert without ever catching a fish. Yet in my own mind I felt at ease, as if all my financial troubles were over, as if at any time I liked I could just run out the Gate and make my fortune. All that spring I continued to haul fishing parties.

Meanwhile just about everything that could float had put to sea. Purse seiners from Monterey, halibut boats out of Puget Sound with names like Helga, Leif Erikson, Gjoa, crab boats and trawlers from Eureka, and salmon trollers from San Francisco, all were fishing sharks. Even rowboats with outboards could be seen far out on the ocean. Many fortunes were made and there were many reports of drownings.

In midsummer, Joe La Rocca bought a new boat, a fifty foot diesel fully equipped that must have cost ten thousand dollars.

"Take the gear off my old boat," he said expansively, "and get out there before it's too late."

But still I did nothing.

Then two misfortunes befell me almost at once. An amendment to a law regarding party boat licensing had been passed. Through some oversight on my part, I'd failed to comply with the new regulations and my license was revoked. That very night when I got home, my wife announced she was pregnant again.

It was already late in October. The shark fishing season, I knew, would soon be over. Yet, once again, with the energy born of desperate necessity, I installed the power gurdy from Joe La Rocca's old boat, got together the necessary fishing gear and, although I had wasted the best of the spring and summer months, I finally took off for Half Moon Bay some twenty miles down the coast where the shark fishing at that time of the year was best. I went alone, figuring to pick up someone there who knew the water. I anchored off the little town of Princeton on the first of November. It was on the second day of that month I first saw Ethan May.

3
◢ ◢ ◢

THE FISH BUYER AT Princeton told me about him.

"If you want somebody that will get you fish," he said, "get this guy May. He's a weird one but he's honest," the buyer went on. "He'll probably make you some kind of damn fool deal, but if he does, take him up. You won't lose. Only you'd better get out there quick because once we get a south blow, you can figure that'll be the end of the shark fishing for this year. And next year they'll probably be making Vitamin A out of sea water or garbage and sharks won't be worth nothin'."

That afternoon I had passed at least fifty boats working along the twenty fathom bank off Montara and Pillar Point. I had pulled alongside several and they told me they had been averaging better than a half ton per boat per day, and that a few of the bigger boats had gone over a ton. Eighteen-hundred dollars in a single day, I had thought, and had been dizzy with the excitement of it all the way in to the anchorage.

"Get hold of him for me," I said. So the buyer got on the phone and called somewhere and in a few minutes was talking to Ethan May.

"Yeah, sure," I heard the buyer say, "a big boat. Maybe good for twenty tons." I couldn't hear May's voice. "OK, I'll tell him," the buyer said. He hung up and laughed.

"You got yourself a deal," he said. "I told you the guy's weird. He says he'll go out for two days with you and you can have the first three tons if he can have all over that. I figure you'll be damned lucky to get a ton this late in the year, so I said OK."

Three tons, I thought. Fifty-four hundred dollars. I lit a cigarette and tried to appear calm.

"A share for each fisherman and one for the boat is the usual thing." I said, trying to appear professional. "How come he makes an offer like that?"

"Who knows?" the buyer said, a little irritably. "He lives alone. He's got nobody. Probably he gets a kick out of playing his hunches. You got yourself a deal so I wouldn't worry if I was you." He concluded abruptly.

"He'll be in on the seven A.M. bus which stops in front of the hotel."

Still in a daze, I left the buyer's office and in the short November twilight, walked out on the pier to watch the boats unload. A long line of them, mostly crab boats, waited in a big half-circle extending a quarter of a mile down the bay. One by one, they came forward and tied up between the mooring floats at the end of the pier so the swells could not smash them against the pilings. The boom from the loading hoist swung out over the fish holds. The men on the boats put slings around the tails of the sharks and the hoist lifted them up in dripping clusters onto the scales on the dock. They were deep water fish, bottom feeding from their sand gills and, as they swung head downward, their air bladders hung like fat red tongues out of their big crescent mouths and their heavy guts pushed forward, swelling out their white, blood-streaked bellies between their big flapping pectoral fins. Hanging that way with their bellies bloated made their long tails look even longer and thinner while their wide set eyes stared sullenly out of their flat, long-snouted, gray-green heads. A man with a broom pushed the blood and disgorged slime into the water while the gulls, darkly white in the evening air, swooped down in screaming clouds upon the reeking refuse.

As I stood there on the pier's end with the dark ammonia-like stench peculiar to sharks—a smell I was soon to know more intimately—permeating the darkening air, I gazed at the clusters of blood dripping flesh that by some freak of circumstances were worth some five hundred dollars a sling load. My revulsion and possibly pity for those disfigured brutes jerked so brutally out of their homes in the sea's depths was overcome by thoughts of the load I would be bringing in myself; of the four or perhaps even better than five thousand dollar check I would get from the fish buyer. I thought of how my wife who at that moment was probably feeding my two undernourished children with leftovers from the previous meal's leftovers would react to such unbelievable good fortune.

And then I thought of Ethan May and the strange proposition he'd offered over the telephone. Suddenly the possibility of three tons of sharks seemed very doubtful, in fact impossible, particularly in view of what the boats were presently bringing in. Looking at it practically, I thought a ton, or at most two, would be almost too good to be true. And if we were lucky enough to catch that much, or even after two days the full three, this Ethan May, whoever he was, would get nothing for his work. The fish buyer had said he was honest. But he had also said he was weird. Weird and honest. A strange combination. Yet, whatever, I'd have to take my chances. And at that moment, I had to admit, they looked good.

The following morning I was awake at two A.M. The Blue Fin was rolling slowly on the long swells that moved in from the ocean. The anchor chain rasped and grumbled in its iron chock. There was no sound of surf, and I judged it must have been a minus tide because of the strong odor of kelp and exposed rocks along the reef. A November chill was in the still ocean air. There was no point in turning out at that hour, so I lay in the bunk watching the cones of pale moonlight through the starboard ports making erratic circles along the opposite bulkhead. A picture had formed in my mind of what Ethan May looked like, a hulking, brutish man with heavy dark hair and a low forehead, probably of southern European origin, who had changed his name. No matter, I thought—and again a feeling of giddiness came over me—I would take the money, however much it was, and buy some property in the City, a house, or better yet a few good units in a decent district. At least with property we'd have a permanent roof over our heads and with the war scare going on, I was sure to get an excellent buy somewhere.

I got up about four thirty, fried a couple of eggs

on the Primus stove in the galley and, after three cups of bitter coffee left from the night before, I rowed over to the pier in the skiff. A cold, clear light suffused the cloudless morning sky above the round black hills to the southeast. The water in the bay was black as was the wide sweep of ocean beyond the reef. A flock of silent gulls, high up and lighted by the sun, flapped seaward. As I walked down the heavy splintered planks on the pier and up over the hard wet sandy beach, the fetid smell of sharks, of sea wrack, of rotted pilings and the high water residue of crude oil was overpowering.

There were some free postcards in the hotel's lobby with a photograph of the hotel, retouched to make it look large and elegant. I addressed one of the cards to my wife and two to the children, wrote a short note to each and left the cards with three cents at the desk to be posted.

I was standing on the hotel porch when Ethan May stepped off the bus at seven o'clock.

The first thing I noticed was the pair of shiny new rubber sea boots he carried tied together and slung over his shoulder. In one hand he held an old black leather suitcase with a piece of cotton clothes line tied around the middle. His other hand was thrust into the pocket of the old flannel slacks he was wearing. He walked over to the foot of the hotel steps and looked up at the porch.

The sleeves of his faded blue sport shirt were rolled up tight above his elbows. He had on worn white sneakers, and he did not wear a hat. His head, which was completely bald, seemed unnaturally white in the early morning light. The paleness of his lashes and eyebrows and the unblinking eyes gave his face a simple, childlike look.

"Are you Ethan May?" I asked, surprised and a little disturbed by his appearance.

Without answering, he took a new cellophaned card from his shirt pocket and handed it up to me. It was his commercial fishing license. Ethan May. Address, general delivery, San Francisco, Age, thirty. Five feet seven. Weight, one hundred seventy-five. No hair. Green eyes. American. Single.

He put his suitcase down, took a small black skull cap with a little tassel on it from his trouser pocket, and put it over his bald head. I walked down the steps and handed him back the license. As he picked up the suitcase again, I could see his wide corded wrist and the heavy muscles under the tanned skin on his firearm. And when he looked up I saw that his eyes were pale green, about the color of seawater under a breaking wave.

From the quiet look on his face and the direct, almost innocent look in his pale green eyes, I could get neither an impression of intelligence nor the lack of it.

And so far, either from shyness or possibly because there was nothing to be said, he had not opened his mouth.

We crossed the highway and started down the beach toward the pier where the skiff was tied. The sun was up. I could feel it burn into the ring of sunburned skin around the collar of my hickory shirt. Back up under the hills, the shadows were still black. The water in the bay and also the ocean beyond had changed to a deep, inky blue. From across the bay, for the first time that morning, I could hear the low moan of ground swells tumbling over the reef and I could see the green and white water rushing in between the black barnacle covered rocks.

May kept slightly ahead of me, walking with long solid steps, his stout legs driving his sturdy body forward, his white sneakers leaving deep prints in the hard wet sand. The big suitcase swung lightly in one hand and the boots bounced against his calves. With each step, the little tassel on his skull cap bounced about like a small rubber ball. From time to time he looked about with a kind of absent-minded interest, down at the wave-washed sand, at the sky above the rocky headland at Pillar Point, out over the dark blue water. He sniffed the air and squinted toward the sun.

"The weather should be good for a couple of

days," he said in a slow, quiet voice, paused, cleared his throat and added, "then it'll probably blow from the south."

Now there was nothing to say to a statement like this. I did not even wonder how he had come to the conclusion there would be a south wind in a couple of days. Ever since I had seen him get off the bus my hopes had been dwindling. The buyer had assured me May was a good fisherman. At the time there was no reason to doubt him. Now I recalled the buyer had been quite abrupt with me. Probably he had sized me up as some young greenhorn and, rather than ignore me entirely, had brushed me off with this fellow Ethan May. As May and I walked down the beach toward the pier, it struck me there was nothing about him except possibly the license he had shown me that had indicated he knew anything at all about fishing. The white sneakers he wore, the worn-out sports clothes, the old suitcase tied with clothesline, the shiny boots which were obviously new, and now this preposterous prediction about the weather all seemed to point to but one conclusion. He was no fisherman and probably knew nothing at all about boats or the water.

Suddenly I remembered the crazy deal he had made that the first three tons were to be mine, and the thought struck me that I might even be stuck with some kind of a crackpot. A feeling of misgiving came over me, and by the time we had climbed up on the pier and were heading out toward the end where the skiff was tied, I felt that I had just lost my one and only chance to escape the misery my family and I had been forced to endure for so long.

The buyer was standing by the loading hoist when we came up. He was talking to the skipper of a big halibut boat from Seattle that was taking on provisions. Above the mewing of the hungry gulls that arced and crossed in a winged maze above the boat, I heard the skipper saying:

"I think the season is pretty near done." He was a ruddy-faced Swede with fine ash blond hair. "We're going up north to Bodega. If there's nothing there, we try it off Fort Bragg. Then we go home."

Whether or not May had heard what the skipper had said, I couldn't tell. He was looking at a couple of small soupfins that had come off the halibut boat and were lying stiff as dry leather in the bottom of a big fish box. The buyer had glanced up as we approached, but gave no sign that he remembered either May or me.

"I'm going up north myself tonight," the buyer said. "One of the big drug outfits bought out the fish company here. They've been doing it all along the coast.

My guess is that next summer they'll get together and knock the price down so low on shark liver it'll hardly pay to go out."

4

♪ ♪ ♪

IT WAS ALMOST EIGHT o'clock when we climbed aboard the Blue Fin. Ethan May took his suitcase below and came up in a few minutes wearing a thick cotton sweatshirt, and he had put on his shiny new sea boots. He did not wear the boots with his belt through the loops, but folded down so that the folds came just above his knees. In a leather sheath at his waist he carried a short bladed knife. I went below and started up the big heavy-duty engine, and when I came back on deck, he had already made the skiff fast to the mooring and was standing by to let go the line.

As I headed the Blue Fin along the reef toward the harbor entrance, May got up a box of bait from the hold and, sitting on the edge of the hatch, his wide shoulders slightly hunched, his powerful fingers moving with quick precision, he began to work the sardines onto the big shark hooks and set them in neat rows around the rims of the tubs. The sun was well up and beginning to warm the air. The sky was clear and what little breeze there was seemed to come from no particular direction. A dozen or more gulls, some gray and white, some speckled brown, hovered over the stern or swooped down close to the deck, screaming and flapping their wings. High above those squabbling by the stern, one big gray-backed bird with a brilliant white breast glided silently through the clear morning air.

The easy familiarity with which May had handled the boat's gear and the way he was getting the hooks baited and the lines in order began to cheer me up. By the time we had cleared the black spar buoy at the end of the reef and the Blue Fin lifted her sharp bow into the long swells moving obliquely in from the ocean, I was whistling a little tune softly above the deep heavy beat of the engine. In fact, I remember exactly what I was whistling—*Josephine*. It had been popular when I had first met my wife; and as I whistled, pictures flashed through my mind, of our wedding at the little church in Sausalito, of the birth of our boy at the county hospital and of our little girl at the University medical clinic. Now there'd be a private room on the maternity floor of St. Francis hospital with big bunches of roses from Podesta and Baldocchi for the new one's arrival.

I swung the wheel over and headed the Blue Fin due west in the direction of some boats a mile or so off shore and stepped out of the wheelhouse to see how May was doing.

Except for the one statement about the weather, May had said absolutely nothing. Now he looked at me with his pale green eyes and, in the same quiet, slow voice as before: "This time of year," he said, "the sharks usually feed along the forty fathom bank." Then he cleared his throat again and added; "Probably they will be on green sand bottom."

My hope that had been running from hot to cold and back, now disappeared altogether. The best fishermen in the area had been knocking themselves out for months getting sharks. They had probably explored every foot of water as far out as they could get lines to the bottom. If there were any sharks on the forty fathom bank, they would be working out there and not close in as they obviously were. I looked down at the tubs. There were nine of them with a hundred hooks in each and all set in neat rows ready to be put down. A fish on every hook, I reflected, would bring in enough money to feed a family of four for ten years. Unbelievable! At the moment I would have been happy to make enough to cover expenses.

May still sat on the hatch baiting the hooks in the last tub, his deft fingers slipping the barbed points of the big galvanized hooks under the gills and down along the backbones of the fat, silver-bellied sardines that were just beginning to thaw from the crushed ice in the bait box. The intent concentration of his pale eyes on his work and the way his black skull cap with its little bobbing tassel was perched right in the middle of his head reinforced my earlier impression of a childlike simplicity. And as I watched him working steadily at his baiting, I got the feeling that he was not as much interested in the money he might make from the trip as he was in just being there doing something. Even if he were weird and dogmatic with his predictions about the weather and the fish, he certainly knew what he was about.

I went back to the wheel, not quite sure what to do. If I'd had any experience at all with sharks, or for that matter with any kind of offshore fishing besides salmon trolling with sport fishermen, I could have made my own decision about where we would put down the lines. As it was, I was pretty much dependent upon him. By now we were far enough out so that I could get a good look around. But I could see no more than a half dozen boats. They were scattered over several miles of a roughly north to south line. Beyond, in deep water, I could see nothing.

I leaned over and shouted through the wheelhouse door.

"We'll try the first set along here," I said with as much authority as I could get into my voice, "anywhere in between these boats. It's probably pretty close to twenty fathoms now." I had no idea how deep it was and felt immediately that May knew I hadn't either.

May did not answer, but went on methodically baiting the remaining tubs. Then he got up, and after washing his hands in a bucket of seawater he had pulled over the side and sluicing down the deck, he went aft with one of the red buoy kegs, a bamboo pole with a flag for a marker, and stood quietly by the stern roller waiting for me to cut the speed. The squealing of the gulls was like a net of shrill sound overhead. Only the big gray-backed bird with the brilliant white breast stayed aloft, passing now and then across the wake, or without the slightest movement of his wings, glided serenely ahead, high above the bow.

When May had dropped the keg, and the bamboo pole had snapped up straight with its little black pennant waving in the light breeze, the new manila line began to pay out smoothly over the stern roller. May made fast a light anchor at the end of the buoy line, and then the main line from the first of the tubs started slowly to uncoil. I stood with my hand on the throttle, watching anxiously as the big baited hooks slipped, one by one, from off the tub's rim and slid across the deck and over the roller. May had taken his knife from its sheath and was standing by to cut the stout three-foot ganions that attached the hooks to the line in case one should foul. Just then he motioned to me for more speed. With a kind of nervous uncertainty, I turned up the throttle. As the Blue Fin jumped forward, the line snapped taut and the hooks began to whip from the tub with an ominous whishing sound and a sharp crack as the sardines hit the water. From the wheelhouse I could see the pale yellow manila line descending in a long flat arc, and hanging below it, the chain of silver flashing sardines, magnified and distorted in the clear, dark water. When the first tub was empty, May, with one quick movement slipped it aside, and the line in the second tub began to uncoil. The engine pounded steadily, the hooks whipped ominously from the tubs. The gulls, screaming in a blurred frenzy, plunged at the sardines on the hooks or made wild sweeps at the bait box.

Suddenly from high above, the big white breasted gull folded his wings and, dropping like a bullet through the cloud of smaller gulls, snapped up a fat sardine that had just swung over the roller. He shook his head and started to take off when I saw he was hooked. As the line went down he flapped his powerful wings and, for an instant, rose into the air, his hooked beak dragging the ganion up with him, and in that instant two small speckled gulls fell screaming upon him, pecking and tearing at his widespread wings until he disappeared in a swirling gray and white bundle beneath the water.

Whether or not May had seen the gull I could not tell. About the middle of the set, he put on another anchor and a third one when the end buoy line went over with its bamboo pole and the flag for a marker. Then he motioned for me to cut the engine.

I was still thinking about the big gull getting hooked and dragged below. However, there was no more reason, I told myself, for getting sentimental over the death of a bird than for the sardine he had attempted to eat. But for the chance turn that got it into the purse seine net, the sardine would now be breeding in the sea or feeding upon some lesser unfortunate who, in its turn should, by like analysis, have my sympathy also.

I switched off the engine and, still standing in the wheelhouse, looked out on the deck. May, who was washing his hands in the bucket of seawater, seemed to have completely forgotten the big set we had just put down. His unlined face, with its clean tanned skin and quiet green eyes, looked relaxed and peaceful. The unconscious rhythm with which he moved seemed in perfect harmony with the sky, the water and the slow rolling deck upon which he stood. And as I watched him, it occurred to me that never in my life had I known anyone who appeared so free of worry and so serenely detached from the harassments of life.

Yet, whether at the time I admired May's complacence or merely envied it, I do not know; but the quiet pleasure he took, not only in his work but in just the simple business of washing his hands, was having a strangely salutary effect on me. The tension in my muscles and stomach that, until then I'd never quite realized was there, slowly ebbed away and a kind of airy lightness began to flow through my body. The curtain of anxiety that as far back as I could remember had obscured and distorted my vision lifted, and a new and surprisingly beautiful world appeared almost magically before me. The late morning sun that normally would have been nothing more than a disturbing reminder of time wasted made a broad silvery track southward, a liquid pathway over which I could easily imagine myself a child again, skipping excitedly toward some divine kingdom in the sky, while all around me the slow, inbound swells flashed and twinkled as from countless bright trinkets in the blue darkness of the water.

With a feeling of unaccustomed delight, I stepped out on deck. The air was warm and soft, and in the silence of the stopped engine I made a surprising discovery. I could feel the Blue Fin floating. I say floating because when the heavy hull, vibrating to the pounding pistons, was moving forward at seven or eight knots, there was no feeling of floating, only a persistent and distracting clamor that numbed the senses. Now as we lay buoyantly lifting and falling on the long swells, the lapping of waves at the waterline, the woody thumping of the rudder post and the muted creaking of planks and timbers, all combined to bring my senses into perfect harmony with the easy motion of the sea around me.

At the time, however, I did not question this curious transition in myself, whether May's influence had wrought the change or if something else, perhaps some natural safety valve, was responsible. The unusual experience of feeling myself fully alive and the unbelievable joy it brought left no room for reflection. With new awareness I gazed out over the water. Close by I could see the buoy keg, bright red and strangely out of place on the wide expanse of blue on which it bobbed, and above it the black flag fluttering languidly on its bamboo pole. Far away and looking no bigger than a period, appearing and disappearing against the pale sky, I could make out the first flag that marked the far end of the line. Between those two flags and stretching over two miles of ocean floor, I knew lay some thousand baited hooks. But the thought of sharks down there, of tonnage, of liver, of Vitamin A, of the war in Europe, of work, of money, seemed to vanish altogether in the cool blue stillness of the day. Even my family, though no more than twenty-odd miles from where I stood, seemed remote as if they were living in another life.

Suddenly I had a deep desire to talk to Ethan May, or possibly not to talk at all, but just sit and eat or maybe smoke a cigarette. I was still standing by the open door of the wheelhouse and May had just gone below. He had taken off his skull cap and put it in his trouser pocket. I followed him down, got the Primus stove going and cooked up some canned stew and made a pot of coffee.

We ate in what I seemed to feel was a kind of friendly silence, with the Blue Fin rolling just a little, the portable table open between us, he sitting on the starboard bunk, I opposite and the soft sunlight through the open ports making slow patterns on the white painted bulkheads. May's black suitcase was open beside him and when we had finished our coffee, he brought out a big almond chocolate bar, broke it, and handed me, I think, the larger half. I still remember, after twenty years, how it tasted, of the pleasant, homely feeling I had while eating it, and of the cigarette I smoked and of May's pipe, that short stemmed, heavy bowled, comfortable pipe he filled and tamped with his thick strong fingers and the way he leaned back on the narrow bunk and puffed contentedly until we went up on deck again to bring in the shark line I'd almost forgotten and that had probably soaked too long or had lost its bait to the big red ocean crabs.

Yet once the engine was going and the Blue Fin's big wheel began to churn up a mound of white water astern and a wide ribbon of wake streamed out of the dark, sparkling water, the troubles, fears and complex uncertainties were back in an instant. It was as if they had never left me. I headed toward the first buoy line, and when the flag was alongside, I slowed down while May brought in the keg with the boat hook. So far he made no indication, either by gesture or expression, of what we might expect to catch. He worked with the same quick efficiency as before, a kind of buoyant cheerfulness in his strong, coordinated body. Now, as the buoy line came in over the starboard roller and around the flat, grooved wheel of the power gurdy, my anxiety was such that I could feel my heart beating heavily in my chest. When the anchor was up, I swung the wheel over and put the bow a few points off the direction of the set and then, with one hand on the wheel and my head through the open window, I gazed down at the mainline that was coming in slowly from off the ocean bottom. But as far as I could see down into the wavering depths, the hooks hung clean and empty on their long ganions. As the last of the set came in, I caught myself, despite my disappointment, watching tensely for the body of the big gull. But by the empty hooks it was evident the crabs had gotten him. When all was aboard, one small male soupfin lay on the deck along with a few red cod, a couple of worthless leopard sharks and some odds and ends of stickle-backs, smoothhounds and a skate or two. May threw everything back except the cod which we could sell, and, of course, the one soupfin which, when I weighed it on a small spring scale, though it was less than thirty pounds was worth more than twenty-five dollars. A whole week's wages at the real estate office! I looked around for the boats I had seen that morning. All were gone. A thin trail of smoke lay low and quite still on the horizon far off to the west. Beyond that, the ocean was empty. And, except for the soundless passage of the long shimmering swells, there was no movement anywhere. Even the gulls that had been with us all morning had disappeared. And standing there on the Blue Fin's slow rolling deck in the middle of that immense blue emptiness with the sun slanting, as it seemed, by the minute toward the sea, I was aware of such an overwhelming sense of hopelessness that had it not been for Ethan May, who with his same imperturbability was coiling up the last of the buoy lines, I would have turned north and headed back to the Gate.

5
⸙ ⸙ ⸙

As soon as the gear was in order May began once more the long job of baiting the hooks. Somehow I think he must have suspected how I felt, for I sensed a subtle change in his movements and, though I may have been wrong, a suggestion of concern on his face that seemed, in some particular way, to indicate tacit sympathy. Of course all this was a long time ago, and my thoughts since then may well have colored the accuracy of my memory. I stepped back into the wheelhouse and turned up the throttle.

"Where to now," I shouted back as cheerfully as I could. May put down his work and came in beside me.

"I think we'll have better luck on the forty fathom bank, off Año Nuevo Island," he said in his soft, slow voice. There was not the slightest trace of resentment in his manner, nothing at all to reflect my failure of the morning. "We can try one set today and then set out again early in the morning." He paused to draw a little circle on the chart and then went back to his baiting.

The white conical tower of the light station at Pigeon Point was visible above the water a point or two to the east of south. A few miles beyond, I could see on the chart, was Año Nuevo. Using my homemade parallel rule I drew a line from our present position to the circle May had drawn and set the Blue Fin on her course. The distance I figured to be about eighteen miles, which would take some two and a half hours. I studied the area around the circle May had drawn. The chart showed the dark, sinuous line at the edge of the forty fathom bank. The legend indicated a green sand bottom, and close by, mud, green mud, brown mud, and occasionally shell. Westward, the ocean floor dropped abruptly and father out configurations of pale blue lines showed depths to nineteen hundred fathoms. Here and there names appeared like Pioneer Sea Valley or Guide Seamount; names that told of some sinister terrain far below the depths of light penetration, peaks and valleys in silent blackness and vast deserts of slimy ooze. I lit a cigarette and waited for the hours to pass. Whatever dreams I had had that morning of making a windfall in the shark business had vanished completely by now. My only hope was that we might catch one or two more to pay expenses. But even that looked improbable.

When May finished baiting, he lined up the tubs, got the keg and bamboo pole ready on the after deck, then washed his hands, folded his skull cap and put it into his trouser pocket and went below. He returned in a few minutes, however, with two big navel oranges, handed one to me and sat down on the deck of the wheelhouse. After peeling his orange and flicking the skins expertly through the doorway and over the side, he parted the segments and ate them slowly, one by one. Then, with his back resting comfortably against the bulkhead, he lit his pipe and began to puff away quietly as if he had no care in the world. After a while he put the pipe away, let his bald head droop forward, and the next moment, despite the pounding of the engine directly below him, was fast asleep.

Suddenly I felt very much alone and was tempted to wake May up on some pretext or other. But there was nothing I could think of to ask him. Then it occurred to me that even if he were awake he probably wouldn't say anything anyway. I leaned on the sill of the open window. There was no wind and the sky was so blue it seemed to pulsate. The water had darkened considerably and toward the west looked almost black. The machine-tooled

straightness of the horizon was so devoid of even the tini-
est irregularity that I found my gaze drifting slowly from
one end of the ocean to the other. Actually, there was no
need for talking, I thought, at least not out there. My wife
and I talked almost all the time. Sometimes we talked all
night long. But as I stood there looking for something to
see on that empty ocean, I could not remember a single
thing we had ever talked about, except possibly our mu-
tual worries over money and even these we hardly ever
expressed in so many words. I ate the orange May had
given me. Remembering it now, that orange was probably the must succulent and sweetest I'd ever eaten. I lit
a cigarette, but since it didn't taste good after the orange
I flicked it over the side and watched it swing aft and dis-
appear into the white furrow of the wake.

And then, still looking out over the water, I began
to think about the little story of the fisherman and his
wife that I had read so often to the children from
Grimm's Fairy Tales. I pictured the poor fisherman quite
clearly, hauling up the big flounder that was an en-
chanted prince and the flounder saying, "I pray you let
me live; what good will it do you to kill me?" When the
fisherman returned for succeeding wishes, I remember
how the sea had changed from purple and dark blue to
gray and was thick, and finally, when he came for his last

wish, how the sea came in with black waves as high as church towers and mountains and all with crests of white foam at the top. And thinking about the fairy tale I had read so often made me think of the children and I felt a painful twinge of guilt. And all the while these odd bits of thoughts went through my mind, and the engine pounded, and the Blue Fin, rolling slowly, moved steadily out toward the forty fathom bank, Ethan May slept.

When Pigeon Point was off our port quarter and I could just make out what looked like it might be Año Nuevo Island with its tiny white sliver of a light tower, May got up from the deck of the wheelhouse, put on his black skull cap and looked out through the window. Then he came over by the wheel and, after glancing at the chart, suggested we take a sounding. I threw the engine out of gear, got out the lead line and put some tallow in the cup at the bottom of the lead. As the Blue Fin drifted in a slow circle, I put the line down. We were in thirty-eight fathoms, and when I brought the lead aboard, there was green mud on the tallow. May took the wheel and headed west, stopping from time to time, while I took the soundings. When the depth showed forty fathoms and green sand was on the tallow, May went aft and let out the buoy line.

6

ナ ナ ナ

I USED TO BELIEVE that time would efface certain memories, or at least take the pain out of them. I see now that this was wishful thinking. Time passes and things change. Outwardly I'm no longer what I was. I eat too much, gain weight. I've gotten soft, lost my hair. My wife, who was once quite shapely, is troubled by a figure problem. Her hair has turned gray. Time passes and things change. But, for the most part, they're happy changes. We do not talk all night as we once did. We come and go pretty much as we please. Healthy love exists between us all, a tranquil kind of love engendered by the freedom from anxiety that springs from the security of affluence.

But these doubts, these ugly shadows. They skulk about. I wait but they do not go away. And then one moment off guard, one little rift, and a whole scene appears before me. It is mid-afternoon, cool, bright with a moving shadow under the lee of the Blue Fin's rust-mottled hull. I feel a slow rolling, driving forward, hear the prolonged S sound of the bow wake, the ominous hiss of the up-flung shark hooks. Ethan May's sturdy figure stands framed against the sky. After twenty years, this scene, and one other, cling obstinately, at times obsessively, defying altogether the effacing power of time, and every effort of will.

We were a good five miles offshore. The white sand beaches had sunk below the rim of ocean. Faintly, I could see the broken segments of yellow cliffs extending to the north and south and out of sight. Long hills, round and brown and parted here and there by wide hazy valleys, faded back into the dim gray peaks of the coastal ranges. The smell of land seemed far away. Over the stern roller, the heavy mainline, with its sardine pendants like silver ornaments, descending at a steep angle and disappearing far below the watery darkness, made me acutely conscious of the eerie depths below. At that moment I had but one desire, and that was not for sharks—I'd given up all hope by then—but to be back in the City, back with my wife and the children, however impoverished we might have been, however dismal the future might have looked.

When the set was down and the last buoy line was

out, we went below for a bite to eat and some hot coffee. As always, May sluiced down the deck, washed his hands, and after folding his black skull cap and putting it into his trouser pocket, followed me into the galley. Nothing seemed to disturb him. The fact that all the other boats had gone, that we had gotten almost nothing on our first set, that we were now far out on the ocean and completely alone with the end of the season almost on us, all of which had put me into a state close to despair, seemed to affect him not at all.

Nor could I tell how he felt about the gull getting hooked that morning. I could only assume that he took that too, like everything else, as a matter of course. He ate the big salami sandwich I put on the table with obvious relish. And when we had finished our coffee, he settled back for a while with his pipe. Shortly he got up.

"We'd better pick up the line," he said. "It'll be dark soon."

"You think there'll be anything on it?" I asked in a voice that must have shown my nervousness.

"Well, I hope there'll be," he said in his slow soft voice. "We just do the best we can."

I started up the engine and headed the Blue Fin back alongside the first marker. May pulled the keg and the pole aboard and the set line followed. I leaned out of the wheelhouse window and squinted down into the water watching as it came up from the bottom. I could see the line bending away into the clear blue darkness and a few bare hooks swinging on the ganions from the taut manila. Then from out of the depths I could see the long, gray-brown body of a soupfin emerge slowly into the underwater sunlight. Further down was another. I jumped back to the wheel, cut the engine to an idle and headed the boat along the line. Then I grabbed a gaff and pulled the shark up onto the deck.

I don't remember how long it took to get the set in, but I remember that it got dark and that either May or I turned on the deck light. Beyond that there was a weird, dreamlike quality about everything, the white light overhead, the quick liquid reflections on the black water, the irregular sput and gurgle of the underwater exhaust, some dim stars rotating in drunken circles and the feel of the steel gaff driving into hard live flesh. And there were strange sounds like grunts and sighs, at once human and unearthly, of fleshy turning and twisting, of the fleshy thud of the axe head, the squeak of rubber boots on blood, the impotent slapping and bumping of heavy bodies from the black hold. Yet through the delirium of twisting, sighs and thumpings, the unreality of steel in live flesh, black blood glistening, the thick ammonia

stench rising and all enacted in that disk of hard light entombed in night sea darkness, a part of my mind, with
machine-like accuracy, was counting . . . one two . . . two
. . . two . . . three . . . four . . . five . . . five . . . five . . .
six . . . until finally four hundred and eighteen . . . four
hundred and eighteen. It was not until I had stumbled
into the wheelhouse and scratched the number on a corner of the chart that I came up out of the depths of what
seemed an evil, exalting trance and, clinging to the wheel,
breathing heavily, I felt for the first time the burning in
my back and in my arms and down through my thighs.

When I heard the hollow thump of the buoy keg
on the deck, I turned up the throttle and, still in a daze,
headed the Blue Fin east toward land. For quite some
while I could hear May moving about and then the
splashing of water as he sluiced down the deck. Presently
he was standing beside me, folding his black skull cap
preparatory to putting it into his trouser pocket. On his
clean tanned face I could detect a slight flush that might
have been excitement. But there was no fatigue, no sign
of weariness. He could well have just finished a brisk
morning walk the way he quietly filled his pipe.

"We can lay in behind Año Nuevo," he said. "It's
a rocky bottom but your big kedge anchor will hold all
right."

He lit his pipe and the sweet, sharp smell of tobacco filled the wheelhouse. "You go below and rest a
bit," he said, and taking the wheel swung it over so that
the three quick flashes that were the Año Nuevo Island
light came up over the Blue Fin's bow. "Thanks," I mum-
bled, embarrassed by my evident exhaustion, but happy
to stretch out for a few minutes. "Thanks a lot."

Below, the heavy stench of the sharks had already
begun to penetrate the galley and the forward cabin. I lay
down on one of the bunks and closing my burning eyes
began immediately to calculate mentally the weight of the
sharks. From what I had heard the males averaged forty-
five pounds, the females sixty. Figuring at fifty pounds
per shark, it would take a hundred and twenty or more
sharks to make three tons. A warm glow spread through
my aching limbs. There were more than three times that
many sharks in the hold. Five thousand dollars! Five
thousand four hundred dollars! And a hundred dollars
added for expenses. Fifty-five hundred dollars. At twenty-
five dollars a week, that would be two years, three years
. . . no, more than four years . . .

I fell into a quick troubled sleep in which frag-
mental events of the day appeared in garbled, shadowy
disorder. Clouds of small speckled gulls descended on the
Blue Fin and were tearing great hunks of flesh out of

some enormous sharks that squirmed on the deck and snapped their huge jaws. A giant gull with gleaming silver armor plate on its breast and giant black-tipped wings had lifted one of the sharks so that it was suspended full length in the air. A long, thin snake was coiled in one of the tubs. Its flat triangular head rested on the tub's rim. A red barbed hook darted in and out of its mouth. And in the middle of all this, his face smeared with chocolate, May lay stretched out on the hatch cover, sound asleep in the dark sunlight.

7
✦ ✦ ✦

WHEN I WOKE UP the Blue Fin was rolling slowly. The engine was stopped and I could hear the anchor chain grinding in its iron chock. May was in the galley cooking something on the Primus stove. He had opened all the ports but, despite the cool breeze and the bulkheads that separated the sharks in the hold from the cabin, the smell was almost too much. I got up feeling dizzy and a little sick to my stomach. May was making up a Joe's Special he had put together from odds and ends—eggs, canned spinach, onions, some leftover rice—he had found in the ice box. A pot of coffee was just coming to a boil. The smell of the food cooking and the good smell of the coffee made me feel better. I got out the folding table, then went up on deck to look around.

The Blue Fin was anchored a few hundred yards to the lee of what looked in the bright starlight like a long low island with some dimly lighted buildings toward one end. The light tower was invisible, but at intervals of about a minute a brilliant white beam near the center of the island illuminated the darkness, eclipsed, flashed twice more, then eclipsed again. To the north of the island I could make out the vague white line where swells broke over a long reef. The low rumble of water, though close by, seemed far away. Either I had gotten used to the shark stench or the little night breeze had dissipated it. Suddenly I thought of all the sharks in the hold and again a pleasant, warm tingling spread through my chest. Ever since we had started pulling the set a strange dreamlike quality had pervaded everything. Now as I stood there on the Blue Fin's deck with the night sea sounds around, the chuckle of a lone gull, the low booming surf, the sharp sweeping cry of a kildeer, the quiet lap of water, and above, the unbelievable brilliance of the November sky, the happy reality of it all began to come through to me. From the bottom of my mind, the magic number fifty-five hundred kept repeating itself, rhythmically, like a drum beat or a pulsing heart.

When I went below, May had his Joe's Special on the table. Suddenly I was hungry, starved. The food was excellent and I ate until my stomach hurt, mumbling comments on both. I sensed May's pleasure at my rude compliments though, as always, I could never be quite sure about anything he felt. While I was drinking my coffee and smoking a cigarette, May got two cups from the galley and an old bent corkscrew. Then he opened his suitcase and brought out a bottle of red wine. The kerosene lamp, swinging a little in its gimbals, threw a soft shadowy light over the cabin. From time to time the thump of a shark could be heard, probably stiff now, rolling against the hull.

"Today is my birthday," May said in his same slow voice, and, after straightening the corkscrew with his strong fingers, methodically pulled out the cork.

"Thirty-one?" I asked, remembering his fishing license.

"Thirty-one," he replied. He filled both cups and pushed one across the table to me.

"Well, congratulations," I said. "I feel like it has been my birthday, too."

We raised our cups in the yellow lamplight and drank. The wine was a rich Burgundy and in scarcely more than a minute I could feel my muscles relaxing and a pleasant drowsiness came over me. I kicked off my shoes and pulled up a blanket. The dishes were still on the table. Since May had cooked the dinner, I knew I should clean things up. But I could not budge. I closed my eyes for a moment. My whole body seemed to float away, and though I could hear May moving about and the soft clatter of dishes, I still could not budge. It was only when I heard the double click of May's suitcase being snapped shut that I managed to open my eyes for an instant. And then, guilty as I felt for not having forced myself up, I had to chuckle at the sight of May's stocky frame clad in a pair of red flannel pajamas, like some little boy in a fairy tale, as he reached up to put out the lamp.

The dream was vivid. I was standing in the wheelhouse with my hand on the throttle. There was a big load of rocks in the hold and on the deck. The rocks were covered with little specks of something that looked like mica and glittered in the bright sun. The hull was down almost to the sheer strake and the after deck was awash. The water rushing in and out through the rocks made a sharp hissing sound. Close by lay a low sandy island, apparently far out at sea. May was standing on a small dune watching the boat pull away. He had on his sweat shirt; his new sea boots were turned down. He held his black skull cap in his hand and was quietly puffing on his pipe. In the dream, it was imperative that I leave him there because his additional weight would capsize the boat. I shouted to him that I would be back, but for some reason, either because he could not hear me or was not interested, he just stood there quietly puffing on his pipe. I shouted again, but this time I could not even hear my own voice. I turned up the throttle slowly so that the Blue Fin would not go down by the stern. As the little island receded, I realized I was crying. But when I wiped away the tears I found great red streaks on the back of my hand.

When I opened my eyes, I could still hear the sharp hiss of water through the rocks and then the softer grinding of gravel on gravel. For a moment I could not disengage the dream from the unfamiliar reality in which I found myself. Then slowly it came to me that the Blue Fin must have swung on her anchor chain and lay in closer to the shore across from Año Nuevo. Little waves, probably after waves from the reef, were washing up on what I could tell now was a shingle beach, rolling the small pebbles and making the hissing sound among the larger rocks. The moon had risen; by its pallid light through the open port, I could see the glass chimney of the kerosene lamp swaying in its gimbals, and again, like on the previous night, erratic circles danced on the bulkhead, the rudder post thumped woodenly and from forward came the rhythmic grumbling of the chain in its iron chock. No sound came from May's bunk, but I could make out the outline of his sleeping figure and even thought I could discern his slow, even breathing. And over everything, like a thick blanket of some noxious gas, lay the dark ammonia stench of the sharks in the hold.

For the first time in what seemed like days, or even months, I thought of my wife and the children. Suddenly I felt a great longing to take them, all at once, in my arms and feel their tender live warmth close to me. Then I thought of how I would break the news to my wife about the fifty-five hundred dollars, and how she would just look at me startled and unbelieving, and then when she saw that I was serious, that I had the signed receipt for the sharks and the amount of money to be paid in cash all stated in writing, of how her eyes would fill with tears. Of course the children would not understand, but they would feel the effects of it soon enough in the good food and the new place to live and in the changed attitude of their parents. Yet, we would have to be careful. Even that much money, though more than I could have saved in a lifetime, could be dissipated all too quickly even on necessities. Actually, it would take four or five times that much and properly invested to guarantee any real security. Fifteen tons would do it. Fifteen tons of soupfin sharks. How odd to be lying awake in the middle of the night in a lonely anchorage mentally balancing the tonnage of sharks against one's future security and happiness. But that was how it was, I thought. Fifteen tons of small gray sharks, and they were all out there somewhere, at that very moment, swimming around, feeding on the forty fathom bank. Yet ten tons of them already were safely stowed in the Blue Fin's hold. Two-thirds of all that I would ever need, and more coming in tomorrow.

Suddenly, like a black shadow, the thought passed over me that three tons belonged to me.

Three tons only. All the rest was Ethan May's and whatever else we might bring in the next day. A kind of silent sickness went through me, a sickness born of envy and fear. But I had more money right now, I reasoned, than I'd ever dreamed of having. This is what I told myself. If it had not been for May, I'd have less than nothing. I would not even have been able to pay for the expenses incurred on the trip to Half Moon Bay. I owed everything to him. But I could not rid myself of the knowledge that there was something like eighteen thousand dollars worth of fish aboard and that better than twelve thousand dollars of that was May's share.

The rumble of the surf on the reef had faded to a low murmur like a far off freight train in the night. The Blue Fin must have turned with the tide change, for the pale dancing circles disappeared quite suddenly. In the darkness, the stench of sharks lay heavy on the dank sea air. What would May do with all the money he would get, I wondered. Would he still live in a little furnished room down in the tenderloin somewhere? For some reason, probably because of the General Delivery address on his fishing license, I pictured him living in a furnished room or in one of those old hotels around Third Street with a public bath down the hall and wooden rockers in the lobby where old men sat and watched the street. And he had no one, the fish buyer said. Most likely his parents were dead or far away in another country. And his tranquil self-sufficiency, that made unnecessary even his need to talk, had probably put marriage completely out. Then what would he do with twelve or fifteen thousand dollars? Gamble it all away? He was a gambler, there was no doubt of that. No one in his right mind would have made a deal like the one he had made with me. And he had made similar deals before and lost. Probably he got a kick out of playing his hunches, the buyer had said. But even if he didn't gamble all his money away, what then? Would he give it away? But to whom? And for what? Certainly it would never go for any useful purpose like feeding and housing a family and getting kids an adequate education. What he'd probably do would be to blow the whole works before the next spring.

This last disturbed me so that I sat up in my bunk and lit a cigarette. Everything seemed so unfair, I thought bitterly. Those who needed nothing always seemed, by some prearrangement, to get everything. Ethan May would probably have been just as happy, just as complacent, if we had gotten no sharks at all. Yet, here he was with more money than he knew what to do with while I, who had a whole family depending on me, came out with a bare fraction of what he would make.

I put out my cigarette and lit another. There must be some way to equalize things. Perhaps I could talk to him, tell him about my situation, about my wife and the children up in the City. He might even be willing to consider making a different arrangement for the next day's fishing. But I quickly discarded the idea. Perhaps, and I wondered about this, perhaps he already knew about me. Or maybe he just didn't care about money and figured I didn't either. One way or another, if he had thought about giving me a larger share, he would already have said so. No, it wouldn't do any good to talk to him, I concluded, and besides, there was something about May that did not invite confidences. Suddenly a picture flashed across my mind of the after deck with its tubs of shark gear, of the big hooks snapping ominously over the stern and the white breasted gull flapping helplessly on the line. An instant surge of fear went through me and I inhaled deeply. The cigarette flared in the dark.

A new thought occurred to me. Everyone had concluded that the season was over, yet we had caught what was probably one of the biggest catches of the year. No doubt we would get more tomorrow. Then what was to prevent me from going out the next day and the day after? No one knew for sure when the weather would change. It could very well continue fair for weeks. And certainly May would be willing, considering what he had already made, to go out for a one-third share, which was common practice. Even if we got a couple of tons a day, in a week's time I would have ten tons or so which, with the three I already had, would give me around twenty thousand dollars. With that much I could manage very nicely. I would invest every bit of it in real estate. In ten years' time the accrued equities would make me independent for life, and in the meantime we would all live decently, like human beings.

I put out my second cigarette and, pulling the blanket up over me, closed my eyes. But I could not sleep, for somehow with the act of closing my eyes, my thoughts, as though held in check by the visible darkness, suddenly went out of control; the events of the day, the gulls, the long lines, the wide shining water, the choco-late, oranges and wine from May's black suitcase, and the dreamlike shark haul under the swinging cargo light all tumbled crazily in my mind. And I was aware too of the low rumble of the surf on the reef, the little waves lapping on the shingle beach, the clanking, thumping and creaking of the Blue Fin, the smell of sharks and, through everything, the soft sound of May's breathing from the opposite bunk.

8

IT WAS POSSIBLY FIVE o'clock and still quite dark when the springs on May's bunk squeaked. A moment later I heard him throw back the blankets and get up. He lit the kerosene lamp and went into the galley, and I could hear the splash of water as he washed his face. I was wide awake, as I had been for hours. My eyes burned and my body ached, but my mind was clear now as though all my thoughts took flight with the yellow glow from the kerosene lamp. While May was getting into his clothes, I got up and, despite my sore muscles, put on my shoes and started the Primus up. The least I could do, I thought, was to get breakfast on since May had made the Joe's Special the night before. I scrambled some eggs with some chopped up Spam, made a stack of toast, set out the oleo and a half-empty jar of plum jam, and poured the coffee.

We sat opposite one another and ate in what, by now, had become an habitual silence, yet a silence that in many ways I was learning made a better conductor of feelings than words. And upon that silence that bridged our separate thoughts, I sensed something not quite right, some shadow of suspicion in May's mind. All during breakfast I had the feeling he was watching me with those innocent green eyes of his, that possibly he was puzzled or curious or even disappointed. No doubt all this was nothing more than a product of my imagination, a projection of some guilt or other. But whatever, I could not bring myself to look up at him and ate my eggs and Spam with my gaze consciously averted.

The sound of the surf had all but disappeared and the Blue Fin lay still and silent as though she were beached. The weather had changed. There was a thickish quality in the air that was not entirely from the settled stench of the sharks. And through the open port a low star glittered fiercely.

Perhaps I was merely suffering the anxiety of a guilty conscience, but the subtle change I'd detected in May's expression continued to disturb me. I was certain with that almost mystic insight that had enabled him to locate the sharks he had seen at a glance all that had been in my mind during the night. No doubt the full

meaning of those oppressive dreams and fruitless spec-
ulations were as clear to him as they were obscure and
confused to me. What satisfaction I'd gotten from my un-
expected good fortune was completely forgotten. The
clearheadedness I'd experienced earlier vanished.

With the Primus going the cabin was quite warm.
Yet I suddenly felt cold. I did not drink my coffee, but
sat with the heavy mug cupped in both palms staring at
the oily film on the thick black surface. The silence, the
unfamiliar lack of motion and the glittering star dilating
grotesquely through the thick glass in the portlight lens
all combined to add to my growing disquietude and
sense of foreboding. Everything around me seemed suddenly strange and unreal. It was as if I'd awakened from
a bad dream only to find myself in the grip of another,
even more disturbing. And, as in a bad dream, an aura
of impending disaster, dark and of unknown magnitude,
seemed to lay like a sinister presence, not only over the
Blue Fin's cabin, but over the whole vessel as she lay dead
quiet at her anchor in the predawn starlight.

Yet I had no cause to feel guilty, I reflected, trying
to console myself. My night thoughts could easily be
justified, not only by my genuinely desperate needs, but
by May's mysterious and possibly suspect deal. As for the
dreams, whatever they might have symbolized, they

were, unquestionably, just garbled reruns of the day's bizarre events and certainly beyond my conscious control. And besides, when the fishing was done and the sharks unloaded, it would be May with his quiet compassion—taking the wheel when I was exhausted, cooking the dinner and even washing the dishes so I could rest—it would be May with his deep inner joyousness and that almost other-worldly serenity who would walk off with most of the profits. If anyone felt guilty, I concluded indignantly, but at once considerably relieved, it should be May.

In spite of my relief, however, I still did not look up. By the light, sweet odor of tobacco smoke I knew May had finished his breakfast. I heard him gather up the plates from the table and set them quietly on the sink, then caught a quick glimpse of his gray sweatshirt as he disappeared up the companionway ladder. If he had suspected anything, either by my expression or behavior, I thought, he certainly did not show it. His lithe, strong body and light step seemed, as always, all innocence and goodwill.

The star was gone from the portlight, and, though the sky was still quite black, I could sense the approach of dawn. My coffee was cold. I put the cup down and lit a cigarette. With May already on deck, probably getting the sardines out of the hold, I knew we'd soon be heading back to the forty fathom bank.

But I felt no desire, or rather, could find no good reason to get up. My thoughts seemed to be groping about for something to hold onto. I tried to visualize the coming day with the sets down and the boat rolling slowly on the long swells, or May leaning back in the shadow of the wheelhouse smoking his pipe, or maybe dozing a bit. But all I could see was the chart with its myriad symbols and long curving lines marking out the seaward edges of these silent black terraces that descended ever deeper into the abyssal gloom.

No sound came from above; no doubt May was sitting on the hatch baiting the hooks, getting himself ready for another big catch, possibly half again what was already in the hold. My stomach tightened unpleasantly. I found myself hoping, almost desperately, that the sharks had disappeared and nothing was left on the bottom but green sand and crabs.

Suddenly I wished I'd never seen a shark, that livers and Vitamin A, my tantalizing dream of wealth and especially May, with his shrewdly calculated deal, had never existed. But despite my wish, I could not rid myself of the shadowy forms that kept twisting and turning in the murky depths of my consciousness.

Goddamn May and his lousy deal! And there was no way out of it, nothing to do all day but pull in May's sharks and watch him get richer. The tightness in my stomach spread to my chest. My throat constricted. Tears welled up in my eyes. And all the while May, serene in his self-detachment and childlike simplicity, was up there on the deck probably smoking his pipe in the fading starlight, completely oblivious to my suffering.

Or was he?

Slowly, and deep in my mind, eerie thoughts began to take shape. Who was this Ethan May, I asked myself. He was weird but honest, was all the buyer had said. And he lived alone. But where alone with no address but a P.O. box and no home or family that he ever mentioned? Where had he come from with those just bought sea boots and a brand new fishing license? How had he known where the sharks would be and that a storm was coming? And where would he go when he left with all his money? The questions came rapidly like an interrogation I sensed was moving, inexorably, toward some ominous disclosure I did not want to know about. What if that mysterious deal of May's were not the long shot gamble it appeared to be or May, himself, the honest fisherman the buyer had claimed he was?

A creepy feeling came over me as tales told to me

in childhood by that ancient, godfearing grandmother of mine emerged from the misty recesses of my mind, whispered accounts of mysterious strangers, God's secret agents, who wandered eternally over the byways and through the outlands of the earth searching out the evil in men's souls, of how they tempted the wicked with visions of gold and precious jewels to expose the greed in their hearts.

Of course all this was pure nonsense, I tried to tell myself, nothing more than an old woman's fears venting themselves in primitive superstitions. But my breathing had slowed almost to a stop and my whole body felt suddenly hollow. Nervously I spread the fingers of one hand on the table as if to find in it some evidence of my innocence. The hand, unwashed since the morning before, was dark with accumulated grime. A thin crust of dried shark's blood still clung to the sides of the fingernails. For a moment I could not accept it as my own. Then slowly, and for the first time, it occurred to my that my hands had always been dirty, grubby and sticky as a child and never quite clean as an adult. In its sordidness, my outspread hand seemed somehow to reflect the values and aspirations, the sickly hopes and dreams I had always lived by.

Suddenly, and with the ineluctable clarity of a revelation, my whole life rose up before me, a bleak montage of fears and failures, of self-deceit and rationalizations, of fantasies of ill-gotten wealth and of whimpering self-pity. And coiled in the depths of this spiritual morass I could see quite clearly the unfounded suspicions that had begun with my first relationship with May and that had culminated in the lethal envy of those malevolent night dreams of mine.

Yet this shocking recognition, this beholding of myself stripped naked and defenseless, instead of destroying me as it could well have done, or driving me deeper into even more secure defenses, was like a resurrection or a new birth into a world devoid of evil.

The yellow flames in the kerosene lamps had begun to pale. Imperceptibly the black shadows on the painted bulkheads faded into the amorphous shades of dawn. The long night vanished, and in the cool morning light all my confusion and guilt, my deadly dreams and hallucinations seemed to vanish with it. I felt suddenly free, and, I believe for the second time in my life, buoyant. From above I could hear the scratchy sound of a bait box being dragged across the deck and then the familiar, sweeping cry of gulls, no doubt circling and swooping over the stern.

As I stubbed out the cigarette that had burned, unsmoked, almost to my fingertips, I thought of my share of the sharks and the unbelievable fifty-five hundred dollars. The upsurge of pure joy was almost more than I could bear. I went into the galley, scrubbed my hands with scouring powder and brown soap, then gathered up the dishes and washed them quickly. Filled with a marvelous new energy I hurried up on deck concerned now as to how May might have reacted to my strange behavior.

As I'd expected, he was sitting on the hatch, busy with his baiting. His skull cap, cocked jauntily to one side, gave his face a kind of carefree, almost cavalier air that was made even more pronounced by the shadow of a beard. Only the tassel, which by now had acquired a personality of its own, hung limp on its string like a little dead puppet.

By the tubs which were already baited, I knew I must have been sitting at the table for more than half an hour. Considering the phenomenally high value of the catch aboard, the lonely anchorage and the still lonelier sea on which we'd soon be fishing, most anyone, and especially May with his acute perception, would have found my prolonged and sullen withdrawal at breakfast, at the very least, suspicious and been on guard. But in the quiet smile that greeted me as I stepped out on deck, I could sense no fear whatever. Not even a slight uncertainty. He seemed pleased to see me. And in his thought-ful green eyes, darker now in the early light, I thought I detected a kind of affectionate concern and under-standing which later, oddly enough, I chose to interpret as forgiveness.

Yet whether I was again projecting my own spe-cial needs into an omnipotent personality I could well have created myself, or whether May, in truth, was all my panicked conscience had revealed him to be, I have never been quite sure. One way or the other, it didn't matter. The last obstacle to my new found joy seemed to have vanished as completely as had my agonizing night thoughts when dawn came. And, for the moment, I thought no more about it. As I went below to start the engine, the tormenting question of how many fish we'd catch or who would make the profit seemed suddenly of no importance. All I could wish for I seemed already to have.

9
✦ ✦ ✦

I HAD ALWAYS TAKEN pride in my ability to get the engine started. But that morning I had trouble. I pulled on the heavy flywheel until my arms were numb. I could not get a single cough out of it. I removed the igniters and cleaned the points with a file, primed the cylinders with raw gas, blew out the fuel line, checked the carburetor, cleaned the sediment bowl and pulled again. But in the pig-headed way old engines have of demonstrating their independence, and always when they're most needed, the fool thing remained as inert as though it were a solid block of iron.

Finally, sweating and exhausted before the day had even begun, I went back on deck. The sun was up and the air kind of muggy. A white haze covered the sky. May still sat on the hatch baiting. He had rolled up the sleeves of his old sweatshirt and the fine blond hairs gleamed like gold filaments on the clean, tanned skin of his forearms. As he bent over the tub with his legs outspread, I noticed his new sea boots were turned down as usual so the folds came just below his knees, exposing the white fabric of the inner lining. When he saw me come up he stopped baiting, washed his hands in the bucket of seawater beside him, dried them on a piece of rag tucked into his belt and went below. A moment later I heard him tinkering with the engine.

Though my traumatic experience in the cabin had affected what appeared to be a permanent change in my whole outlook, the eerie feeling I'd had about May was still with me. As I leaned against the wheelhouse smoking a cigarette, I found myself listening with mixed feelings to the dry sucking of the pistons as May spun the flywheel. I wanted to hear the engine start, yet at the same time I half hoped he would fail just as I had. For at this time, any failure on his part would have been proof enough for me of his fallibility and hence assurance of his humanity. To see him come up frustrated and as beat out and greasy as I was, if nothing else, would dispel, I thought, the superstitious fears that had carried over from my frightening revelation.

Suddenly I remembered the chocolate and the orange and how he'd taken the wheel the night before so

I could go below and rest, and the wine he'd opened for his birthday, and the red pajamas that had made him look like a little kid, and all at once I felt embarrassed for even having such thoughts inside me. I flicked my cigarette into the water and went down into the engine room again.

Apparently May had gone through the same routine as I had, checking the fuel line, the carburetor and the igniters and pulling on the flywheel. Now he was leaning against the hull looking at the engine with what seemed to me, and for the first time since I had known him, a perplexed frown. His face was sweating and his arms were streaked with grease. And somehow, seeing him leaning against the hull unable to do anything made me feel better. I crawled in beside him and together we stood staring at that stupid hunk of metal that looked for all the world like some impudent brat defying its elders.

Suddenly, just as though the engine had been playing hide the button with us, we both found the trouble at once. The battery clamp had come loose from the terminal. With a shout, I snapped the clamp back where it belonged and May, almost at the same time, gave a heave on the flywheel. The engine started instantly and chugged away as smooth as you please. We went back on deck, both of us laughing kind of quietly at ourselves. And though nothing further was said, the final barrier between us dissolved away.

Soon after we'd pulled up the anchor, the old Blue Fin, her engine idling, was rounding the south end of Año Nuevo Island and heading back once more toward the forty fathom bank.

The ocean, despite its flat, oily surface, looked swollen. The early sun through the haze had a slightly yellowish cast. As we cleared the tip of the island, I noticed the light was still on. During the night, its diamond flash had dominated the darkness. Now, in the daylight, it looked weak and ineffectual with a pale red tint in its owl-like lens as it winked out its cycle on top of the white-painted skeleton tower.

I was standing at the wheel thinking rather dreamily of how it would be to fish with May on a permanent basis, of going south with him in the summer for albacore and broadbill, then working north for sharks if they were still in demand. Yet, though I was thinking about this and at the same time was pleasantly aware of the Blue Fin's heavily laden roll as she entered the ocean swells, the island with its rock rimmed beaches ringed by tidal spume and brown sea grasses and its lonely light tower kept intruding with dark persistence into my consciousness like the memory of a place I'd only dreamed of.

Suddenly all my good thoughts vanished and I found myself irresistibly drawn back to a disturbing experience I'd had when I was a child.

I was eight years old at the time. An aunt of mine was going with some fellow who had worked as a lighthouse keeper on Unimak Island up in Alaska. From the stories he told me, it must have been one of the most desolate places in the world, with nothing but rocks along the coast and some kind of tall grass inland. The weather was either so foggy you couldn't see anything, or it was blowing a full gale. The light station and the bleak promontory on which it stood was known as the Roof of Hell. On his annual visit to San Francisco he would usually bring my aunt little gifts from up there, some of which she gave to me, like a colored grass Indian basket, a pair of moccasins made of wiry haired white seal skin (I could still remember the rawhide smell) and some mounted walrus tusks with fine, blacklined etchings of dogs pulling sleds, old sailing ships and some Eskimos spearing walruses. He would tell me about the big Kodiak bears he had hunted, about fishing for giant crabs and migratory salmon.

But the story that impressed me most was the one about a big Japanese freighter that had been abandoned in a storm in the Bering Sea. The wind had driven her on the rocks not far from the lighthouse on Unimak Island. When the storm was over he climbed aboard and looted it of cameras, guns, binoculars, no end of food-stuffs, and even a couple of crates of Christmas tree ornaments so that, just for the hell of it, he had said, he and the other two men at the station cut themselves a tree and celebrated Christmas in the middle of August.

As might be expected, I was pretty much carried away with all this and thought of nothing but getting up there myself. But when I asked him if he would take me with him sometime, he just looked me over and said that that was no place for a skinny little kid like me, but if I ever got bigger and got some beef on me he might give the matter some thought.

I remembered quite clearly how helpless and frus-trated he made me feel when he told me this. As a mat-ter of fact I was so filled with rage that, had I been strong enough, I would have killed the lighthouse keeper with my bare hands. In fact, for a long time after I had fan-tasies of doing just that.

Probably because of the impending change in the weather, the usual flock of excited gulls, sweeping and crying over the stern, was nowhere in sight. I opened the window and listened. Faintly from the rocks on the seaward side of Año Nuevo came the short, hollow bark of a lone sea lion. It was the only sound of life.

May had gone back to his baiting as soon as we had gotten under way. His wide shoulders and heavy arms seemed to fill up his old sweatshirt so that the rounded outline of his powerful muscles could be seen clearly beneath the worn gray cotton. The little black tassel on his perfectly centered skull cap bounced from side to side as he worked, but seemed to have lost all its former gaiety.

By eight o'clock, or thereabouts, we were back in the vicinity of the forty fathom bank. The water, with its faint yellowish cast near shore, now turned to a kind of ominous green. Except for the long low swells, lifting and falling as if in a feverish sleep, there was no movement, at all. We took our soundings and when the tallow on the lead showed green sand and the depth was right on the forty mark, I brought the Blue Fin around to a southerly course and May put out the first buoy keg with its bamboo pole and black flag for a marker.

Soon the long set started, hissing ominously as on the day before. Only now I detected an even more sinister quality in the accelerated uncoiling of the blood dark manila as it slithered upward and out of the tubs. In fact, as I remember quite well, everything around me seemed sinister, the pearly haze, the thick morning air and the tumid seawater. And the oppressive closeness of the sky along with the complete dispersion of the familiar and, in its way, comforting hard-lined horizon gave me a feeling of being entombed. I found myself consciously breathing deeper. Even so, I had trouble filling my lungs. But all this, I thought, was probably nothing more than the after effects of my earlier confusion and would soon pass away.

When the baited hooks began their headlong plunge, May, after removing the hatch cover, went aft with his unsheathed knife and stood by the stern roller ready to cut any of the hooks that might foul.

The Blue Fin pounded along with hardly a roll, though now and again the bow, catching a swell just right, flung a low spray that disappeared aft with a muffled splash. No shoreline was visible through the haze, but for the first time that morning I felt a faint breeze through the window that was not from the forward motion of the boat. Fortunately it had come just in time to blow the stench from the open hold away from the wheelhouse. Yet the breeze, though no more than a whisper, started me thinking of May's prediction about the weather. Again, as in the cabin, a creepy feeling came over me and a kind of numbing cold spread through my

chest. My stomach too began to give me trouble with little burning pains and rolling cramps down low. I turned
and looked back at May, half expecting to see some
awesome transfiguration or even, hopefully, to discover
that he was not there at all and that the entire experience
was nothing more than a frightful dream.

But there was no change whatever. May was still
standing by the roller balancing himself easily with one
foot on the deck, the other resting lightly on the comb-
ing. Except for his gray slacks tucked loosely into his sea
boots, and his quaint black skull cap with its bobbing tassel, he could have been the model for some Winslow
Homer "Portrait of a Fisherman." Despite my rampant
fear and upset stomach, at the sight of his sturdy figure
there, his discerning eyes concentrating on the rapidly descending shark line, I was aware of an immediate sense
of calm.

Feeling pleasantly sure of myself, I was about to
return to the wheel when I noticed that something was
wrong. Since I was heading south, the keg with its marker
flag should have remained due north by the compass. Instead, it was moving slowly in an easterly direction which
could only mean that it had broken loose from the buoy
line. Though I knew we could manage with one float, for
some reason the sight of the keg drifting off that way dis-

turbed me. I left the wheelhouse, and shouting back to May, pointed toward the keg that was quite small by now but still bright red against the water. But apparently May was already aware of what had happened. He turned, and shrugging unconcernedly, said in his usual quiet voice that we could get along all right with the remaining keg and went back to tending the line.

In spite of his reassurance, I could not rid myself of the uneasiness I felt at the loss of the buoy keg. For the remaining time until the last buoy went over, I kept thinking of the set stretched out two hundred and forty odd feet down in that vast silence and deep gloom with one of its lines cut and the buoy, indifferent and insensible, drifting away and out of sight over the ocean. Though it was not unusual for me to worry unnecessarily about things of little consequence, my concern for the lost keg was out of all proportion to its importance. It even occurred to me that some secret part of my mind might possibly be busy with things I knew nothing of. However, once the engine was stopped and May and I were sitting at the table drinking coffee and eating the last of the bread and some tough-edged Swiss cheese, my uneasiness left me.

"The sharks might hit pretty well today," May said when he had finished eating. He leaned back on the bunk and puffed on his pipe. "I think they know what goes on up here. They know when the weather will change and when feed will get scarce. Probably they have some kind of extra sense we don't know about."

It was the longest single statement I had heard May make. His voice was unreservedly warm, almost chatty, as if he'd finally accepted me as his friend. Suddenly it occurred to me that, quite probably, he'd been as uncertain of me as I had been of him and, until he knew me better, had confined himself to pertinent observations, to the business at hand. He opened his old black suitcase, rummaged about for a moment, and came up with a table of writing paper and a new yellow pencil.

"We have enough bait for one short set after this one," he said. "Then we'd better get back before it blows." He broke the cellophane wrapper on the tablet and, carefully squeezing it into a ball, tossed it into the paper bag he had set out for garbage.

Somehow this change in May seemed to clear away the last vestige of mystery surrounding him, revealing, no more nor less, the simple fisherman his license had claimed him to be. With immense relief, I realized I was no longer afraid.

I was reflecting on all this yet at the same time considering the prospect of still another set following the one still to come in. A thousand hooks and another half a thousand more. For the next five or six hours, I pictured myself working in a state of exhaustion hauling in these squirming tons of soupfin sharks. The hold would be full and they'd be all over the decks and probably down in the cabin too. They'd represent more money than most men ever saw in a lifetime. Yet when I was all through, I'd get nothing, absolutely nothing for all my labor. And there wouldn't be another chance tomorrow or probably ever again. There was no doubt about it now, the weather was changing.

Suddenly, like the cellophane wrapper in the garbage bag, I felt myself squeezed into a tight ball. With a rush of anger all my night thoughts returned. I lit a cigarette and flicked the still burning match on the deck.

"This whole damn deal was no good to begin with." My voice was tight and I could almost feel the pallor on my face. "I must have been nuts to have agreed to it."

Anger surged up into my throat. For the first time in my life I didn't want words, but some kind of violence. Then suddenly I could feel the deep flush burning in my cheeks. I glanced at May. He had not even looked up. He opened his tablet on the table, adjusted the black lined paper under the top sheet and, with an expression of serious concentration in his pale green eyes, began printing something in large capital letters. When he had finished with his writing, which turned out to be only his name and address at some hotel on Bush Street, he carefully tore out the paper and, weighting it with a box of Kirby hooks, looked over at me with an expression of such ingenuousness and goodwill that I wondered if possibly my impulsive outburst of a moment before was just a figment of my imagination.

One way or another, it was a disturbing little scene, and I was glad when the Blue Fin was under way again and we were heading toward the black flag that marked the set's end and May was setting the tubs in a row alongside the power gurdy preparatory to bringing in the line.

10

✓ ✓ ✓

THE LITTLE BREEZE WAS strong enough now to dimple the tops of swells and to make the flag flutter on its bamboo pole. As we approached the keg, my head suddenly began to pound and my grip on the wheel got weak. It lasted only a moment and, I suppose, was caused by my thinking about the sharks that might already be on the line. Despite the fact that none of them would belong to me, once I got to thinking about them, my mind seemed to turn immediately into a regular calculating machine. A thousand hooks, I thought. One every fifth hook. Two hundred sharks times fifty pounds would be ten thousand pounds, divided by two came to five tons, multiplied by eighteen hundred would be nine thousand dollars. I went over all this several times, savoring the taste of the final figure which, because of other probabilities such as a shark on every fourth hook and then every third, increased progressively to something like thirty thousand dollars. Then I began to think about May again. I pictured the Blue Fin loaded. We were heading back to Princeton. I was at the wheel and May stood beside me smoking his pipe.

"I've been thinking," I imagined May saying in his quiet voice, "that maybe you'd want to sell the Blue Fin."

"I'd be willing to sell her," I said. "I'd even be glad to. But it's this way. I have a wife and two kids up in the City and there's a third one coming. I'm not much of a fisherman, but if I didn't have the boat I'd have no way of making a living."

May kept puffing away on his pipe. His familiar sympathy was almost palpable. Finally he said, "I'll make you a deal. You let me have the boat and I'll give you my share of the sharks."

"But that would be more than five times what she's worth, and about fifty times more than I paid for her," I said. "You wouldn't be getting much of a deal."

But when he insisted, saying he had no need for the money, I agreed to let him have the Blue Fin. By the time I'd gotten the check with its five perforated figures from the fish company and was heading back to San

Francisco on the night bus, the keg was alongside and
May was pulling it aboard with the boat hook. In an instant, my little fantasy vanished.

I threw the engine out of gear and stood by the
wheelhouse door watching the buoy line come up. The
little breeze, steadier now and blowing from due south,
felt warm on my face and a little moist. Probably a good
wind was blowing high up for here and there big patches
of blue came through the milky haze that had covered
the ocean all morning. The line, snapping little sprays of
water, sped upwards in a businesslike manner, silent and
tight as a bow string, as May, with his ever-turned down
boots, widespread for balance, received it from off the
power gurdy and coiled it in neat hard circles on the
deck. When the small kedge anchor, its flukes and shank
dark with slime-green mucky sand and exuding the re-
pugnant smell of some strange decay, came over the side,
the first shark could be seen turning slowly in the murky
water.

Once more, as on the night before, a dreamlike
quality came over everything. The long gray snout of the
hooked shark shot up from the water, the spatulate pec-
torals flapping like grotesque ears, the distended belly
showed white in the translucent darkness and then, with
no pause whatever in the relentless, beltline motion of

the thick manila, the whole length of the slow-thrashing, muscular body was dragged out and, with the aid of May's heavy steel gaff, slid through the two vertical guides of the starboard roller. Then May, in what seemed but a single, uninterrupted movement of his strong body, slit open the throat, disengaged the hook and kicked the squirming soupfin clear of the incoming line. I stepped back quickly into the wheelhouse, shoved the gear lever forward and brought the Blue Fin about so that the line came in on the lee side a few points off the starboard bow. I set the throttle at a slow idle and went back on deck to help May.

No sooner was the first shark aboard than another was coming over the side. And then another. Without even noticing the rancid blast from below, I began throwing the big, twisting fish into the hold. I ran, dragging the sharks by their tails. I skidded, fell, leaped up and ran again. I counted, not to myself now, but aloud, shouting out the numbers in a chanted beat. And still they came, like from the magic salt mill, a steady, unending flow. In no time at all the hold was full. Sharks spilled out and covered the deck. Once I grabbed May's gaff and, leaning far out, sunk the steel hook deep into live flesh. The thrashing weight unbalanced me and I was half over when May's hand, like a vise on my arm, pulled me back.

I fell against the wheelhouse biting air, then was up again and away. In the open hold heaped up sharks writhed, their tails slapping softly, blood sheathed bellies revolving, abrasive, sand-gray and violet backs arching and twisting, crescent, serrated mouths agape in their strange and silent dying. Across the deck dozens more rolled about. Blood-black, phlegmy slime clung to the gunn'ls and sideboards. In the scuppers the bodies of young sharks, disgorged from pregnant females, squirmed weakly like soft, blind tadpoles. Forward beyond the heavy sideboards, a big one twisted and snapped itself into the water. I snatched up the axe and in a frenzy danced about, battering in the heads of every shark that moved. And all the while my skinny body, incited by some demonic fire, darted this way and that, scraggy bearded, uncut hair flying, two days accreted filth on pants and shirt, leaping, squatting, smashing, killing and shouting out numbers in a shrill voice, all the while May's apocalyptic figure, unperturbed, deliberate and infallible, stood bigger than life, by the grooved iron wheel of the power gurdy, all certitude, all rhythm, a procession of dependabilities like the diurnal tides or the equinoxes.

The set was in and May was clearing away a space for the tubs when I finally began to look around and take notice of things. No less than a thousand soupfin sharks

filled the hold, the forepeak and the entire deck from forward of the wheelhouse to the area May had cleared just
aft of the hatch. I stumbled inside and threw the engine
out of gear, then leaned against the wheelhouse and,
with my arm dangling limply, gazed over the monstrous
cargo that shortly would be hoisted, slingload by slingload, onto the pier at Princeton, weighed in and evalu-
ated at some forty-five thousand dollars. Yet at the
moment, I would have given up everything, my share of
the catch and the remote possibility of any of May's
share too just to sleep, to sink down right where I stood
and drift off into utter forgetfulness.

"We still have time for one short set if you feel up
to it," May said, studying the water and the sky to the
southwest. He had just finished sloshing his arms and
face with seawater from the bucket. Now he shook the
water off his hands and came over to the wheelhouse
looking as clean and fresh as if he had just bathed. "It
probably won't blow much until around dark." His
voice was as quiet as ever. There was no sign of weariness either in his movements or expression, or, any sign
of special satisfaction about the forty thousand or so he
had made in less than two days. The fact that there were
still some working hours left seemed, at the moment, to
be his only concern.

The thought of going through the ordeal of another set, even a short one, seemed more than I could take. Besides, I thought bitterly, I would still not get a cent more than my original amount. And then, and for the first time that day, a quick and terrifying image of the big white-breasted gull with its gray-white body twisting in the water passed like something cold across my brain. I flicked my cigarette over the side.

"Well," I said in a thin voice, "I guess we'd better get them while we can."

I did not look at May, but out over the ocean. Except for a few swiftly moving clouds, the sky had cleared. The water, for some reason, had changed to an inky black.

May immediately began getting the set ready. First he separated five of the tubs and, after cutting the line, made the free end fast to the kedge anchor. Then he got out the last of the sardines and started to bait. There was nothing now for me to do, so I went below and put on a pot of coffee. While I waited for the water to boil, I sat down at the table and lit another cigarette. After a couple of drags I stumped it out, scraped off the burnt end, and lit it again. The smoke felt hot in my throat and besides, it was making me sick. But since I didn't want to put it out again, I just sat there holding it and flicking off the ashes. From up forward came the soft thump of a wave against the hull. The Blue Fin lurched a little, then righted herself. I glanced up through the open scuttle. A small cloud bundle, crossing under the sun, turned the sky as dark as a winter twilight.

May's sheet of writing paper lay where he had left it on the table. I pushed aside the box of hooks and studied the big, carefully printed letters that filled the entire space between the guide lines. It looked like the efforts of a child learning to write, simple, diligent and unsuspecting. Yet at the same time I could feel there something ultimate, something just beyond my reach but in some way discernible. And looking at it, at the child's simple efforts, I could see May's strong fingers working away, his pale green eyes concentrated and serious, yet neither shadow nor flame. And then I saw him all at once, a composite of remembrances. And seeing him that way, with the mid-afternoon sun fading and brightening and the Blue Fin lifting and falling more and more sharply gave me such a quick and poignant feeling of sadness that I had to wipe my eyes with my blood stiffened sleeve to clear away the start of tears. In a moment, the whole feeling passed. Yet I continued to sit there, puzzled and at the same time embarrassed, still flicking the ashes off my unsmoked cigarette and I could only explain my strange melancholy away by the fact that I was probably getting a little hysterical.

The coffee came to a boil, foamed over the sides of the blackened pot and, before I could reach it, put out the flame. I poured in some cold water to settle the grounds and was fumbling around cleaning up the mess when May came below. His face was as placid as ever. He had washed off his sea boots so that the black rubber glistened. Even the fabric lining of the rolled down tops had been well scrubbed.

He took off his skull cap, folded it neatly and slipped it into his trouser pocket before he sat down. There was nothing left in the locker but a half box of salted crackers and the remains of some peanut butter. I put these out on the table along with a couple of cups of the steaming, iodine-colored coffee, and sat down opposite him. But again, as at breakfast and on deck a little while before, I could not look up at him.

By the time I got back in the wheelhouse and May had taken his position aft by the stern roller, the entire aspect of the water had changed. The sea had become the ocean with its cool smell of distance and its vast, curving emptiness. I swung the Blue Fin about as the little wind that had picked up came in off the starboard bow. Through the windows that had already caught some spray, I could see here and there along the crests of the dark hills rolling up from the southwest, white tongues snapping skyward with sibilant whisperings, eerie in that big silence, then falling off, making white foam patches down the lee slopes. Though it was still early afternoon, the sun seemed to have gotten smaller and the sky darker. And just above the horizon to the south and west, a low cloud bank, like a weld on the seam between the sky and the water, was now visible.

The area May had cleared was so cluttered from gear that he was forced, in order to keep from stepping into the tubs, to stand with one foot on the gunn'l and the toe of his other foot in one of the scuppers. Since we had but one buoy keg left, he picked up the anchor that was made fast to the end of the set line and, motioning me ahead, tossed it out over the stern with no buoy line. The heavy iron stuck with a soft clunk, the line snapped taught, and then the big hooks, as though suddenly inflamed into fiendish action, leaped hissing from the rims of the tubs, whipped through the rollers and into the waves.

I took a quick check on the compass, then looked out again to the southwest. The cloud bank was higher now, lead gray and flat on top. In the distance, the water looked lumpy, with a kind of confused turbulence as though something were going on below. Close by low, fast-running waves had begun to build. They came on erratically, veering this way and that, yet maintained a general course somewhat oblique to the direction of the big swells. The sun seemed to have drawn back deeper into the sky and to have shrunk to half its normal size. At that moment a wave struck up forward. The Blue Fin shuddered, lunged steeply and then the heavy spray crashed with the sound of a dropped barrel on the cabin deck. I pulled the wheel hard to starboard and then turned quickly to see how May had made out.

Nothing had changed. The blood-black line uncoiled with the same angry haste, the upflung hooks hissed evilly in their short fast trip through the rollers and May, bracing himself by some extraordinary muscular counterbalancing, stood poised, hardly swaying, as the stern swung up over the water then fell sharply back. Poised that way with his sheath knife in his hand and his head thrust a little forward, he looked like the cast figure of some classical hero portraying, by means of this quickly changing backdrop, two alternating views of man, the one, intense and alert, a tight spring, in the midst of rushing water, flying hooks and wild, churning wake; the other, when sharply silhouetted against the clear dark sky, a lofty ascendance that could almost have achieved some sort of omniscience or otherworldly purity except for the little black tassel bobbing and tumbling about as merrily as ever linking the two together and making them one.

Suddenly the sky and all the ocean darkened. It lasted only a moment and then it happened. I saw it first only as an obscure movement like a quick shadow or maybe even a thought or a feeling. Yet when I saw it, it was as though I had known all along exactly how it would be, as though I had had a working drawing somewhere in my mind all the time. The rolled down top of one of May's boots had brushed against a tub and a hook had slipped over the cotton fabric lining of the creased edge. It was just lying there. And then four things happened almost at once. My hand flew to the throttle. Automatically my foot went to the reverse gear lever. My mouth opened to shout. And then I froze. I could not speak. I could not move. I could only stare, paralyzed as the big hooks whipped savagely from off the tub's rim, one second per hook, not more and not more than five seconds to the hooked boot. I thought about nothing. I'm sure I thought about nothing. My mind had stopped. Then, as in a dream, a nightmare, the boot rose from the deck, not high, but just as though May were stepping over the stern and out upon the waves. His arms spread wide, his head turned slightly as if to speak. Only nothing was said, nothing at all. His lightly bearded face was as calm as ever. Only now it was gentle. Suddenly the line tangled. The tub leaped off the deck, crashed between the vertical rollers and exploded, scattering its wooden staves in all directions. Then with a soft, wet snap, the line parted.

With a violent surge of energy, I shoved down the reverse gear lever and opened the throttle wide. My heart pounded. Thin whining noises came out of my throat. The Blue Fin trembled and the bow began to swing. I leaped across to the door of the wheelhouse and looked over. Deep in the waves I could see the vague twisting bundle of gray and white that was May's sweat-shirt and the bald top of his head and then the frayed end of the line, waggling away and out of sight. The black skull cap, top down and partly filled with water, was already half a boat's length away. I threw the engine out of gear and stumbled out onto the heaped up sharks on deck. The spot where May had gone down was lost in an instant. There was nothing anywhere, nothing at all but the silent inbound passage of the waves. A cool, steady wind was blowing now. There was no smell to it, only the feeling that it had come from a long way off, an unspeakable distance, from nowhere and going nowhere.

Suddenly I began to shake, my legs inside my bloody dungarees, my skinny, aching arms, my head, my shoulders. I shook inside. Then my insides seemed to turn to water. My knees went limp and I slipped down quivering upon the deep layer of sharks. For a moment I felt nothing. Then slowly I could feel the abrasive hides, the hard dead flesh beneath and then the viscous slime that enveloped everything and was oozing through my clothes and over my skin. I got up and staggered back into the wheelhouse, holding my hands far in front of me. A clean damp rag lay folded neatly beside the compass box. It was May's rag. I picked it up and began to clean myself. Soon the rag was thick with slime. I wadded it into a ball and flung it over the side, then went back to the wheel. A strange quiescence came over me; all feeling seemed numb or dead. Yet I could think quite clearly. I studied the sky. A few ragged clouds, forerunners of the great dark bank now high above the horizon, sped eastward. Probably it was one of these that had caused the momentary darkness a while before. The wind was blowing harder now, and the swells, with their mountainous crests and deep, black valleys, were traversed by row upon row of fast moving waves. I pulled the wheel over and, with the Blue Fin rolling heavily under her huge load of sharks, headed back toward Half Moon Bay. At that moment, another cloud crossed the sun and blotted out everything. Then, just for an instant, a picture flashed into my mind of the long and empty darkness ahead.